SALLY AND THE SCIENCE FAIR

Written by Aubrey Cressman

SKU: 371723V1P

It was a morning to remember. The morning two days before the big day, the science fair competition! To prepare for the big day, Sally the scientist needed to set up her very important experiment (or VIE for short)!

Sally was studying the affect of different types of light on plants. Before experimenting, however, Sally needed to state a hypothesis.

Sally wondered how to write a good hypothesis. A few minutes later, she remembered that a hypothesis statement is written in the "if, then, because" format. That's what she needed to model her hypothesis after.

After some thinking, Sally decided on her amazing hypothesis statement. It said "If a parsley plant is put under natural sunlight for two days, then it will grow taller (she wanted to say enormous, but that isn't realistic in this experiment), because plants produce food with sunlight."

9

Now that Sally finished her hypothesis statement, she needed to know and fully understand her variables before she moved on. This is because some variables you absolutely can't change if you want the experiment to be valid (and if you want to be able to use any of your research later).

Sally stated "My controlled variables are the plant species, the soil, and the temperature of the environment they are in. My independent variable is the light that they are in. The parsley will either be under led lights, sunlight, or in a dark room. My dependent variable will be the reaction of the plants. My control group will be a parsley plant that lives outside and must withstand the elements."

Now that Sally has written her perfect hypothesis statement and identified her different variables, it's time to move to the next phase of her science fair project. EXPERIMENTATION! This, to some scientists (including Sally), is the most fun and inertesting part of science fairs and science in general.

Sally set up all of her beautiful plants, then she went to bed for the night. She slept soundly, but all she could dream about was three things. Her science project, her future as a scientist, and what college she would go to.

After a good night's sleep, Sally woke up nice and refreshed and ready to finish her experiment!

Sally hurried down the stairs to check on her plants and took observations to share at the competition!

She went to the science fair with all parts of her observations and research. She rushed out of the house making sure to remember everything she found. She also wrote her conclusion on the topic.

23

The conclusion she decided upon was that the light was helping the plant grow taller, and this proved her hypothesis valid. She wrote that down in her journal.

After everything was set and she had all materials needed to present, she went to the science fair to present her findings.

She presented to all of the judges that she noticed the parsley in natural sunlight grew one centimeter in two days. She also showed them the hypothesis and conclusion, and all of her variables. When she finished presenting, the judges let her know that she could wait for the awards in thirty minutes, or she could leave and come back for the awards.

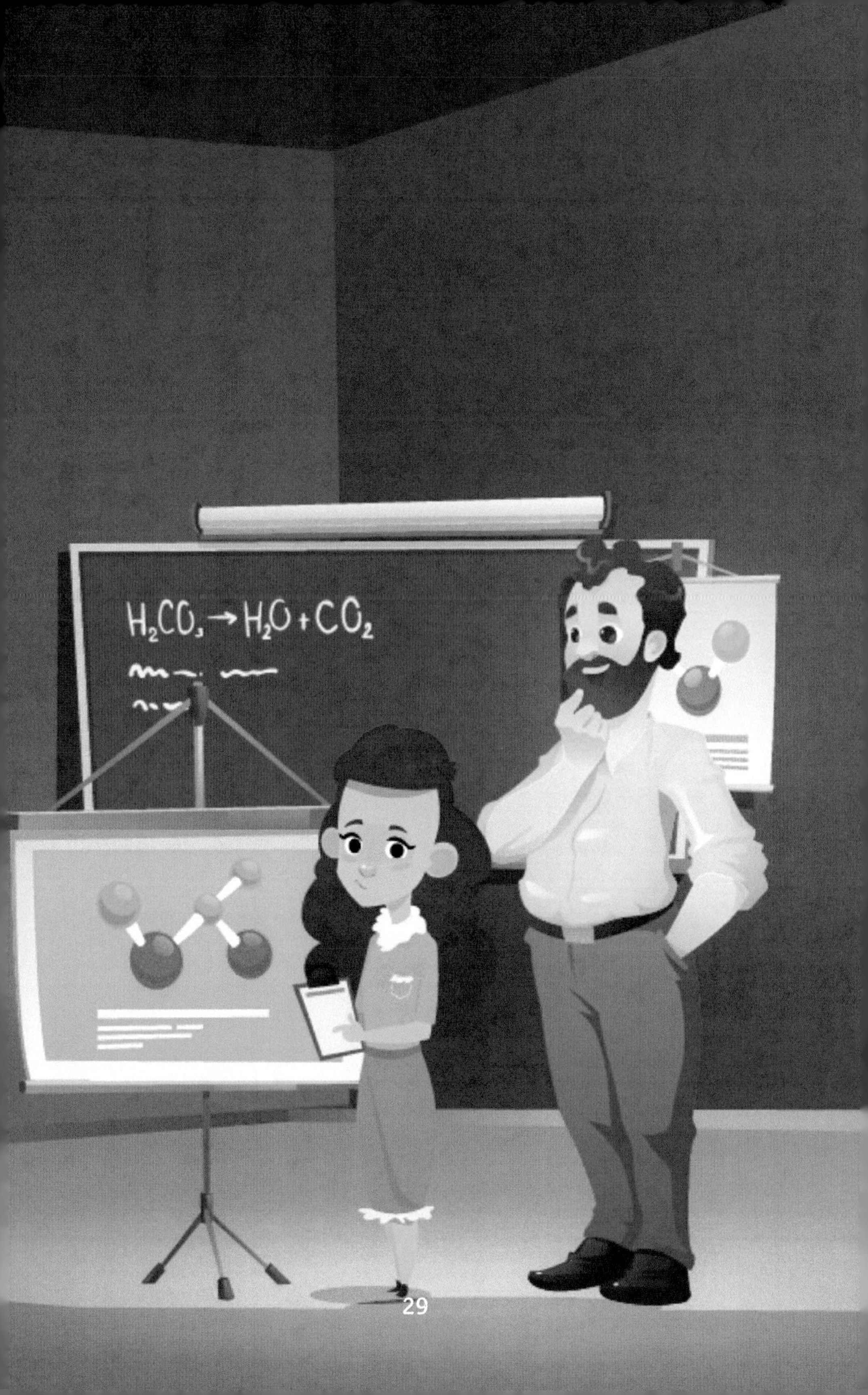
$H_2CO_3 \rightarrow H_2O + CO_2$

Sally decided she would stay and wait the agonizing thirty minutes. Sally was full of anticipation when waiting for the judges to decide, but before she knew it, they were ready to present the awards!

Sally crossed her fingers as third place
was announced, squeezed them even
tighter when second was called, and
even tighter when the announcer
called "SALLY IS OUR FIRST PLACE
WINNER! Congratulations Sally, you
earned it!"

Sally was overjoyed when she realized that she won the science fair competition, and she came home thinking "What am I going to do next year?"

Made in the USA
Middletown, DE
21 December 2023

46661391R00020